# CLASSIC
# BIBLE
## STORIES

Rhona Davies

illustrated by

Tommaso d'Incalci

Contents

# A WONDERFUL CREATION

In the beginning there was nothing at all.

Only God was there.

God spoke, and then there was light in the darkness.

God created snow-topped mountains and deep blue seas. God covered the land with tall trees and scented flowers.

God made the spinning earth, the red hot sun, and the silvery moon. God scattered stars across space.

God filled the sea with fish and the sky with birds, bees, and butterflies. God created animals that crawled on the land. God made people like himself: caring, thinking, feeling, able to love and to be loved.

God was pleased with everything he had made. It was very good.

Everything created by God is good.
1 Timothy 4:4

# ADAM AND EVE CHOOSE

Adam and Eve lived and worked in the Garden of Eden and they were happy.

God asked Adam to choose names for the creatures he had created and to take care of them. God filled the garden with all kinds of delicious fruits and vegetables, and Adam and Eve could eat anything they wanted, except from one tree.

"Eat and enjoy the fruit of all the trees except the one in the middle of the garden. If you eat from the tree of the knowledge of good and evil, you will die," God said.

One day the serpent crept up to Eve and whispered in her ear.

"Did God tell you not to eat from this tree? Look how good the fruit looks. You won't die if you eat this fruit. You will know everything. You will be like God himself."

Eve looked at the tree. The fruit looked delicious. She took a big, deep bite. Then she gave some to Adam.

Suddenly, Adam and Eve knew what they had done. They didn't feel the same any more. They had disobeyed God. They knew how it felt to betray someone and to feel guilt, and they hid from God, their creator.

God made them clothes to wear from animal skins and sent them away from the beautiful garden.

—◦◦◦—

Love the Lord your God, obey Him, and remain faithful to Him.
Deuteronomy 30:20

# NOAH'S ARK

Noah loved God. But the people around him lied and cheated; they hurt and killed one another. They forgot all about the God who had made them, the God who had made everything.

"I am grieved that I made the world," God said to Noah. "I am going to flood the earth with water, and wash it clean."

God gave Noah careful instructions about how to build a huge boat, called an ark. It had to be large enough to keep Noah, his family, and all the different kinds of animals safe. Noah cut down trees and made planks of wood. He hammered in nails and made the ark just as God had told him. Then he covered the ark with thick, sticky tar to keep the water out.

People watched and wondered, but they all thought Noah was crazy to be building an ark.

When it was finished, Noah gathered food for all the animals to eat. The creatures came to him, male and female of every kind of bird and animal, and Noah found room for them on his ark.

When everything was ready, it began to rain. Noah, his family, and all the animals were safe inside the ark. Then God closed the door behind them.

For forty day and forty nights, the rain came down and flooded the earth.

He gazes on all the inhabitants of the earth from His dwelling place.
Psalm 33:14

# THE FLOOD AND THE RAINBOW

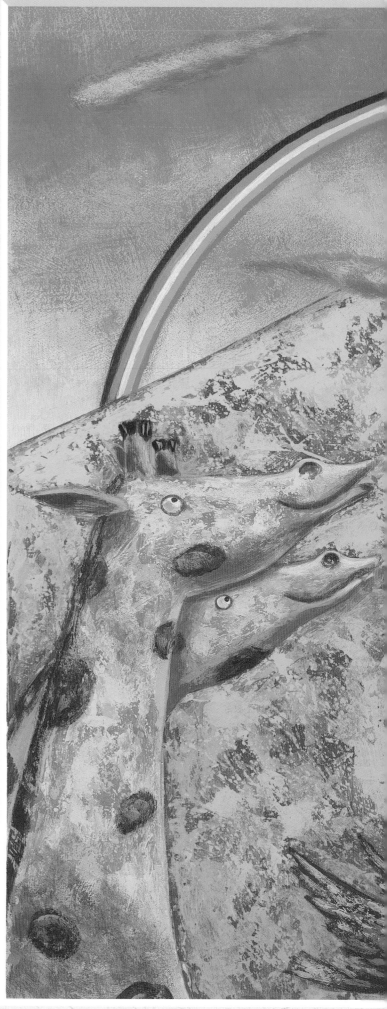

When the rain stopped falling, the ark floated on the flood waters.

After some time the waters began to go down and the ark came to rest on a mountaintop.

When the earth was dry again, God told Noah to open the door. The animals ran free and made their homes on the new land.

Noah thanked God for keeping them safe from the flood and watched as a bright rainbow colored the sky.

"When you look at the rainbow," God said, "it will remind you that I will never destroy the earth by a flood again."

He is not man who changes His mind.
1 Samuel 15:29

# ABRAHAM'S JOURNEY

Abraham lived in the city of Ur. One day God spoke to Abraham.

"I want you to move from here and go to live in the land I will give you," God said. "I will show you where to go and will provide you with a new home. I will bless you, and your family will be the start of a great nation."

"We must pack up our things," Abraham told Sarah, his wife. "We must go to the place where God leads us."

So Abraham and Sarah began their journey with their servants and their camels, with their sheep and their goats.

They walked by day, and each night they stopped and camped in their tents. They did not know where they were going, but Abraham knew that God had promised to be with them wherever they went.

At the end of a long, long journey, they reached the land of Canaan. "This is the land that I will give to you and your children," God said. "It is a beautiful land where you can graze your animals and have all that you need."

Abraham thanked God and rested from his journey. He put up his tent to make his home in the land God had promised to give him.

Those who have faith are blessed with Abraham.
Galatians 3:9

# Abraham trusts God

Abraham and Sarah had no children of their own. They were old now, and Abraham wondered how he could be the start of a new nation without a child.

"I will look after you," God promised. "I will give you everything you need!"

"But Lord God," said Abraham, "what I really need is a baby boy."

"I promise you will have a son of your own," God said. "Look up at the sky, Abraham."

Abraham looked up. The sky was full of stars, twinkling in the darkness.

"Can you count the stars?" God asked.

Abraham shook his head.

"One day there will be as many people in your family as the number of stars in the sky!" God said.

Abraham trusted God to keep his promise.

Some time later, Sarah found she was expecting a baby. She gave birth to a lovely baby boy. They called him Isaac.

Isaac was a very special baby. Through him, God would give Abraham grandchildren and great grandchildren, the start of a new nation.

Trust in the Lord with all your heart.
Proverbs 3:5

# Jacob's Favorite Son

Jacob had a big family. He had twelve sons and one daughter. Out of all of them he loved his young son Joseph best of all.

One day, Jacob gave Joseph a very special present. It was a beautiful, brightly colored coat. Joseph was pleased. He wore his beautiful coat as often as he could. He liked to show it off.

Joseph's big brothers were jealous. They saw how much their father loved Joseph. But they did not love him. He was bossy and boastful. One day, Joseph's big brothers were out working, taking care of their father's sheep.

"Go and see how your brothers are," his father said. So Joseph set off, wearing his beautiful coat. His brothers saw him coming.

"Here comes Joseph!" groaned one of them.

"I've had enough of him!" said another.

"Let's kill him!" said a third. "No one will know. We could say he's been eaten by a wild animal!"

"No, don't kill him,' said Reuben, his oldest brother. "Put him in this empty well."

As soon as Joseph got near, his brothers grabbed him. They tore off his beautiful coat and threw him down into the well.

Soon some traders passed by on their way to Egypt.

"Let's sell Joseph," the brothers decided. "Not only can we gain some money for him, but we won't have to see him again." So Joseph was sold as a slave in Egypt. But God had plans for Joseph. Even there, God was looking after him.

---

I will not leave you or forsake you.
Joshua 1:5

# PHARAOH'S DREAMS

Joseph went to work for a man named Potiphar. Joseph worked hard and his master thought well of him. But Potiphar's wife told lies about him, and Joseph was imprisoned.

Then one day, the king of Egypt had his baker and his wine-taster thrown into the prison. Both the men had strange dreams. But Joseph knew that with God's help, he could understand what the dreams meant. Joseph told them that the wine-taster would get back his job, but the baker would be executed.

It all happened just as Joseph had said it would.

"Remember me!" said Joseph when the wine-taster was released.

Two years later, the king of Egypt had strange dreams that troubled him. The wine-taster remembered Joseph.

So the king had Joseph brought to him. The king explained his dreams about seven fat cows being swallowed up by seven thin, bony cows, and seven ripe ears of corn being swallowed up by seven thin, sun-scorched ears of corn.

"God is sending you a warning," Joseph explained. "There will be seven years of good harvests followed by seven years of famine. You must store up food in the years of plenty so that the people can eat when the harvests fail."

The king of Egypt was impressed with Joseph. He gave him the job of making sure there was food for everyone's needs. Joseph became the most important man in Egypt apart from the king himself.

When the famine came, God made sure that Joseph was there to help not just the Egyptians, but also his people in Israel.

—◦✦◦—

You planned evil against me; God planned it for good.
Genesis 50:20

# THE BABY IN THE BASKET

The land of Egypt was full of God's people, the Israelites. But they were no longer free people; they were slaves.

The new Pharaoh worked the people hard, but he was afraid they would rebel against him. So he decided to kill all the baby boys.

When Jochebed's baby son was born, she hid him. Her baby was a gift from God. But as he grew, Jochebed began to be more and more afraid the soldiers would find him.

His sister Miriam watched her mother weave a basket. Then she watched as her mother covered it with tar to make it watertight. Then she went with her mother as she put the baby boy in the basket and hid it in the papyrus reeds on the bank of the River Nile. Miriam hid too ~ but she watched to see what would happen to her little brother.

Pharaoh's daughter saw the basket. She asked one of her servants to bring it to her. She lifted the lid to see what was inside. The baby boy was crying.

"You are one of the Israelite babies," she said gently. "Don't cry."

Miriam came from her hiding place and offered to bring her mother to look after the baby for the Pharaoh's daughter.

"I will call the baby Moses," the princess said to Jochebed. "Look after him. When he is old enough, he can live with me at the palace."

~◦◦◦~

They saw that the child was beautiful, and they didn't fear the king's edict.
Hebrews 11:23

# TROUBLE IN EGYPT

Moses knew that the Egyptians treated God's people badly. When he became a man, God wanted Moses to speak to the king.

"Tell Pharaoh to let my people go!" God said.

Moses was afraid. He didn't want to go. But he went with his brother Aaron.

The king listened — but he needed his slaves. He refused to let the people go. So God sent plagues on Egypt.

First all the water in the Nile turned to blood.

Then there were frogs, gnats, and flies.

The cattle died and the people broke out in sores.

Hail fell like stones from the sky.

The crops were eaten by locusts.

Then an inky darkness covered Egypt.

Finally the oldest child in every family died.

"All right," said Pharaoh. "You can go!"

---

You called out in distress, and I rescued you.
Psalm 81:7

# CROSSING
# THE RED SEA

The Israelites had not gone far when the king of Egypt sent chariots to make them return.

The Israelites had reached the shores of the Red Sea when they saw they were trapped, with the Egyptians behind them and the sea in front of them.

"Don't be afraid," Moses told the people. "God will save us."

Moses stretched out his hand across the sea. A strong wind stirred up the waters until a path appeared so the Israelites could walk across on dry land. When the Egyptians tried to follow, the waters returned. But God's people were safe on the other side.

The waters saw You; they trembled.
Psalm 77:16

# DAVID AND THE KING

David was the youngest of eight brothers. The three oldest brothers were soldiers in King Saul's army. David was King Saul's armor bearer. He played the harp for him when he became depressed.

When he was not with the king, David looked after his father's sheep in the hills around Bethlehem. Sometimes he killed lions or bears with a stone thrown from his sling. David trusted God to look after him.

One day, David's father sent him to see his brothers. As he walked among the soldiers, David saw they were very frightened. Goliath, the Philistines' champion soldier, was challenging them to fight ~ and Goliath was huge!

"Who will come and fight me?" the giant shouted.

No one stepped forward. No one wanted to fight Goliath, except David. He saw that Goliath was making fun of God's people.

King Saul offered David his armor, but it was too big for him. He offered David his sword, but it was too heavy. Instead, David picked up five smooth stones from the stream and went out with his sling to fight the giant.

David didn't go because he was brave. He went because he knew God was greater than the lion and the bear ~ and greater than Goliath!

—⟡⟡⟡—

"Not by strength or by might, but by My Spirit," says the Lord.
Zechariah 4:6

# DAVID AND THE GIANT

When Goliath saw that the Israelites had sent a boy to fight him, he was
angry. He thought David had come to
mock him.

"You have a sharp sword," David
shouted. "But I have the living God
on my side! Soon everyone will know
that there is a God in Israel who looks
after his people."

David put a stone in his sling,
whirled it around his head, and aimed
it at the giant. Then David watched as
the giant fell heavily to the ground.

The Philistine army turned and ran.
The Israelite army cheered. David was
right. God really was on their side!

With God we will perform valiantly.
Psalm 60:12

# JONAH RUNS AWAY

"Go to the people in Nineveh," God said to the prophet Jonah. "Tell them to stop doing evil things or they will be punished."

But Jonah didn't want to go to Nineveh. Instead he boarded a ship going in the opposite direction, laid down, and fell asleep. A storm blew up while the ship was at sea. The sailors knew they were in danger.

"Wake up!" they shouted at Jonah. "Pray to your God or we will all die!"

Jonah knew that the storm was his fault.

"Throw me overboard!" Jonah said. "Then you will be safe."

The sailors threw Jonah into the sea. The wind dropped and the sea was calm. A huge fish came and swallowed up Jonah whole. He sat inside the belly of the fish for three days and nights – and thought.

"I'm sorry, Lord!" he prayed. "I should have done what you asked me to do."

Then God caused the big fish to spit Jonah up on to the land.

"Go to Nineveh," God said. And this time, Jonah went.

Jonah told the people of Nineveh that God loved them and that they must stop doing wicked things. The people of Nineveh listened and were sorry. They stopped their evil ways. And God forgave them.

―⊙IIIO―

Do not be afraid of anyone, for I will be with you to deliver you.
Jeremiah 1:8

# Daniel is Thrown to the Lions

Daniel lived in the land of Babylon. He had been taken from his home far away and made to work for King Darius.

Daniel loved God and prayed to him three times a day. The king saw that he was honest and hard-working, and rewarded him with an important job in his kingdom. But there were men in Babylon who wanted to make trouble for Daniel.

"You are such a great king!" they said to King Darius. "You should make a new law so that for the next thirty days, no one can worship anyone but you. Anyone who breaks this law must be thrown into a den of lions!"

The king thought it was a good idea and made the law. But Daniel worshiped God, just as he had always done, and prayed three times a day.

The plan had worked. The men knew Daniel loved God more than his life. Now the king had to punish him. Daniel was taken to the den of lions and left there to die.

The king could not sleep that night, but the next morning he went to the lions' den. "Daniel!" he shouted. "Has your God been able to save you from the lions' teeth?"

"I am here, my king!" replied Daniel. "God sent an angel to close the mouths of the lions."

Then King Darius made a new law.

"From now on," he said, "everyone must worship Daniel's God!"

―⦅∞⦆―

They dug a pit ahead of me, but they fell into it!
Psalm 57:6

# MARY'S BABY BOY

Mary was engaged to be married to Joseph, who was a carpenter in Nazareth. One day the angel Gabriel came to Mary.

"Don't be afraid," he said. "God is very pleased with you. You will have a baby, God's only Son, and you will call him Jesus. He will bring peace to the whole world!"

"I want to do whatever God wants," Mary answered.

Some time later, Mary and Joseph traveled to Bethlehem to be counted by the Romans. Everyone had to go to the town where their ancestors were born.

Bethlehem was bustling with people, and soon it became clear that there would be no room where they could stay.

Mary was tired from the journey and knew that her baby would soon be born. When the innkeeper offered them his stable, they were pleased to have somewhere for her to rest.

That night, Mary gave birth to a baby boy. She wrapped him in strips of cloth and made a bed for him in a manger.

During the night, shepherds came to see Mary's baby. They had seen angels praising God out on the hillside who told them that Jesus, the Savior of the world, had been born in Bethlehem.

My spirit has rejoiced in God my Savior.
Luke 1:47

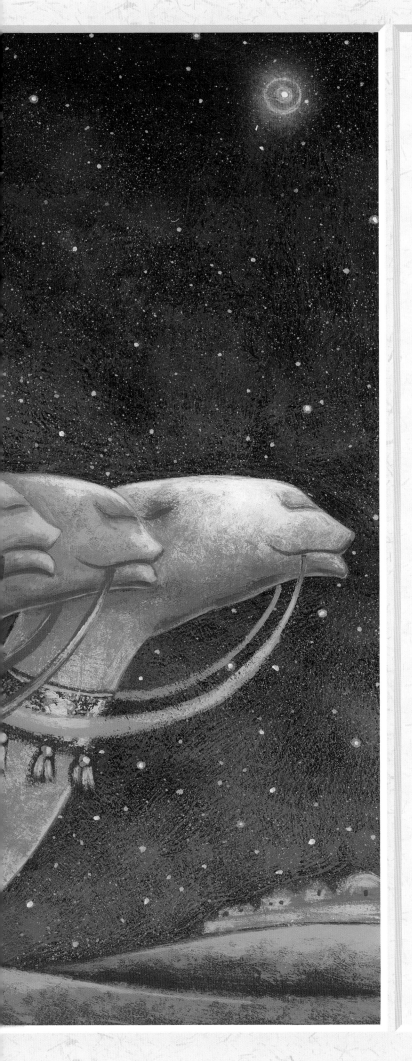

# TRAVELERS FROM THE EAST

Far away, in another country, wise men saw a new star in the sky.

"It means a new king has been born," one of them said. "Let's go and find him," said another.

"We must take gifts and go to worship him," said a third.

The wise men set off on a long journey, following the star.

They stopped in Jerusalem, but King Herod could tell them nothing about the baby king. Then they followed the star to Bethlehem where they found Mary with her child. They gave him their gifts of gold, frankincense, and myrrh, and they worshiped him.

Let all kings bow down to him.
Psalm 72:11

# JESUS, THE TEACHER

When Mary's son was grown up, he chose twelve men to be his disciples. Then he started to teach the people all he knew about God and about the best way for people to live their lives.

"The people who are happy are those who know how much they need God's help and forgiveness," Jesus said.

"If someone hurts you, be kind to them. Go out of your way to help everyone, even your enemies. It's easy to love people who already love us. God wants us to be different.

"Learn to love God more than the things you own. Learn to love other people more than money. One day moths or rust will destroy your belongings on earth. Make sure you have stored up treasure in heaven where nothing can destroy it!

"Don't worry about what you will eat or drink, or what clothes you're going to wear. Look at the wild birds. God makes sure they have enough to eat. Look at the beautiful flowers growing in the fields. They do not work or dress themselves, but God has made them beautiful. God cares even more about you.

"Put God first in your life, and he will make sure that you have everything you need ~ and much more besides."

No man ever spoke like this!
John 7:46

# THE STORM ON THE LAKE

Jesus climbed into a boat to sail across Lake Galilee with his disciples. They had not sailed far when he fell asleep, rocked by the motion of the boat. Then the wind began to blow harder. Rain clouds moved quickly across the sky. The sails flapped. The waves crashed against the sides of the boat and tossed it high in the water.

Jesus' disciples tried to wake him. "Help us!" they shouted over the noise of the wind. "We're going to drown!"

Jesus stood up.

"Be quiet!" he shouted to the wind. "Be still!" he shouted to the waves. The wind stopped howling. The sea grew calm again. The men in the boat were amazed. Jesus had power over the wind and the waves. He spoke – and they obeyed him.

Glory and power belong to our God.
Revelation 19:1

# THE HUNGRY CROWD

Jesus told the people about how much God loved them. He showed them how to care about each other. Jesus healed people who were ill. After they had been with Jesus, the blind could see, the deaf could hear, the lame could walk. So when Jesus went into the countryside, a large crowd of people followed him. They all wanted to be with Jesus.

When evening came, Jesus knew that everyone was hungry.

"Where can we buy food for these people?" Jesus asked Philip, one of his disciples.

"For all these people?" Philip asked, amazed. "It would cost far too much money!"

Just then, Andrew, another of Jesus' disciples, came to him.

"This little boy has offered to help," Andrew said. "But he has only five small barley rolls and two little fish."

Jesus smiled at the boy and took the food in his hands.

"Tell everyone to sit down," Jesus said.

Jesus thanked God for the food he had been offered, then he broke the bread and the fish and shared it with his disciples. Then they shared the bread and fish with the people sitting on the grass. Everyone began to eat.

There was enough for all the people there, and his disciples collected twelve baskets full of what was left over. More than five thousand people had been fed that day by Jesus. It was a miracle.

—◦◦◦◦◦—

The person who gathered little did not have too little.
2 Corinthians 8:15

# THE GOOD SAMARITAN

One day, a man came to Jesus and asked, "How can I please God and live with him for ever?"

"What does it say in the law?" Jesus asked him.

"Love God with all your heart, and love your neighbor as much as you love yourself," the man replied. But then he asked, "Who is my neighbor?"

Jesus told him a story to answer his question.

"A man was traveling from Jerusalem to Jericho. On the way he was attacked by robbers, who stole everything he had and left him dying at the side of the lonely road.

"Some time later, a priest came that way. He knew the man was there but pretended not to see him. He crossed to the other side of the road and walked on. Another holy man came along later. He saw the wounded man, too, but went on his journey without stopping to help him.

"Finally, a man from another country came along. He ran to help the man as soon as he saw him. He cleaned his wounds, put him on his own donkey, and took him to the nearest inn, where he paid the innkeeper to look after him till he was well."

Jesus looked at the man who had asked the question. "Who do you think was a good neighbor in that story?"

"The one who helped the wounded man," he answered.

Jesus said, "You will please God if you behave like him."

—ommo—

If your enemy is hungry, feed him. If he is thirsty, give him something to drink.
Romans 12:20

# JESUS HEALS A BLIND MAN

Bartimaeus could not see. Day by day, he sat by the side of the road and held out his begging bowl as the people walked by.

One day, Bartimaeus heard many voices laughing and chattering — the sound of a huge crowd of people approaching. "Who is there?" he shouted. "Tell me, what's happening?"

"Jesus is coming!" someone answered him.

Bartimaeus knew all about Jesus. Jesus talked to people about God. Jesus performed miracles. "Jesus! Help me!" shouted Bartimaeus over the sound of the crowd.

"Be quiet!" someone answered.

"Jesus!" shouted Bartimaeus again.

"Stop shouting!" said someone else.

But Jesus had heard Bartimaeus. "Tell him to come here," Jesus said.

"Jesus is asking for you," said a kind voice. Bartimaeus threw off his cloak and scrambled to his feet, put out his arms and felt his way through the crowd.

"What do you want me to do for you?" Jesus asked.

"I want to see!" said Bartimaeus.

"You believe that I can help you," smiled Jesus. "Go! You can see."

Bartimaeus opened his eyes. He could see the faces of all the people around him. He could see the bright sunlight. He could see Jesus smiling at him. He had been healed!

Jesus turned to go on his way. Bartimaeus joined the crowd and followed.

---

You love Him, though you have not seen Him.
1 Peter 1:8

# THE LITTLE TAX COLLECTOR

Zacchaeus had heard that Jesus was coming to Jericho. He wanted very much to see him. Zacchaeus was a tax collector, a very rich man. But because Zacchaeus kept some of the tax money for himself, no one liked him. The people called him a cheat.

Zacchaeus stood at the back of the crowd lining the street, but because he was not very tall, he could see nothing but the backs of everyone's heads. And because he had no friends, no one would let him through.

So Zacchaeus decided to climb up into the spreading branches of a fig tree. He saw Jesus walking along the road, talking to the people around him. He saw Jesus approach the tree. He saw Jesus looking up into the branches.

"Hello, Zacchaeus! Why don't you come down so I can come to your house today?" Jesus said.

Zacchaeus scrambled down the tree. Jesus wanted to be his friend!

After Zacchaeus had spent some time with Jesus, he went out and spoke to the people.

"I'm sorry I have taken more money than I should have," Zacchaeus said. "I want to give lots of my money to the poor, and I will give back to anyone I have cheated even more than I owe them!"

Jesus smiled. Zacchaeus would never be the same again.

---

Where your treasure is, there your heart will be also.
Matthew 6:21

# The last meal

Jesus and his twelve disciples met together in an upstairs room in Jerusalem, just before the Passover feast.

Jesus took a basin of water, knelt down in front of each of his friends in turn, and started to wash their feet. Peter protested. He did not want Jesus to do a servant's job.

"You must let me wash your feet," said Jesus, "or you cannot be my disciple."

"Then wash my hands and head as well!" Peter said.

"There's no need," said Jesus. "Only your feet are dirty. I am showing you how you must serve one another. You must not be afraid to follow my example. Then others will know that you are different ~ that you care about each other."

As they ate together, Jesus told his disciples that this would be their last meal together. He had made enemies among the religious leaders; soon he would be betrayed by one of his disciples; soon he would die. Then Judas left the room and went out into the night.

Jesus thanked God for the bread and broke it into pieces.

"This is my body, which is given for you," he said. "Remember me whenever you eat together like this." Then Jesus picked up a cup of red wine. "This is my blood, shed for you, so that your sins can be forgiven."

Jesus' disciples ate and drank with him, but they did not understand what he was telling them.

<hr>

He is always able to save those who come to God through Him.
Hebrews 7:25

# FRIENDS RUN AWAY

Jesus took his disciples to an olive garden called Gethsemane.

"Wait here while I pray," he said to them. Peter, James, and John went with him a little further, then they also stopped.

Jesus walked away so he could be alone, and he fell to his knees. He was very sad. "Father, I want to do all that you ask of me. But if it's possible to save me from the death that lies ahead of me, please help me now."

Jesus went back to Peter, James, and John. They had fallen asleep. Again Jesus went away to pray. Again they were asleep when he returned. Jesus prayed for a third time, alone in the garden.

"Could you not even stay awake with me for a little while?" Jesus asked when he returned.

They all looked up as they heard the sounds of a crowd coming through the garden. Judas walked up to Jesus – and kissed him. It was the signal for the men to rush forward and arrest Jesus.

They marched him away to the house of Caiaphas, the high priest, so that they could put him on trial.

But his friends ran away and left him.

Jesus was passed from the high priest to Pontius Pilate, the Roman governor, even though Jesus had committed no sin and they could find no crime to accuse him of.

---

When reviled, He did not revile in return.
1 Peter 2:23

# DEATH ON A CROSS

A crowd waited outside to hear what Pontius Pilate would do to Jesus. But Jesus' enemies had made sure the crowd was full of their supporters.

When Pilate asked the crowd what he should do with Jesus, they cried, "Crucify him! Crucify him!"

So Pilate let the soldiers take Jesus away. They dressed him up in a purple robe and put a crown of thorns on his head. Then they beat him and spit in his face. They took him away to the place of execution outside the city walls and crucified him between two thieves.

He laid down His life for us.
1 John 3:16

# THE EMPTY TOMB

Jesus died on the cross. He was taken down before the Sabbath started and was buried in a tomb. A large stone was rolled in front to seal the entrance.

Early on Sunday morning, two women who were some of Jesus' friends went to the tomb. They had brought oils and spices so they could anoint his body properly. But when they got there, they saw that someone had rolled the huge stone away from the entrance. The tomb was empty. Jesus was not there.

Then an angel spoke to the women.

"I know you are looking for Jesus," the angel said, "but he is not here. God has raised him from the dead, just as he told you. Come and look for yourself ~ then go, and tell all his friends that he is alive!"

The women were both afraid and overjoyed at the news and at the angel. Then, as they went from the garden, they met Jesus and fell at his feet, worshiping him.

"Don't be afraid," Jesus said. "Go and tell my disciples that I am alive and I will see them soon."

The women ran with the news.

"Jesus is alive! We have seen him with our own eyes!"

The Lord God will wipe away the tears from every face.
Isaiah 25:8

# THOMAS BELIEVES

Jesus' disciples knew that he really had risen from the dead. But Thomas had not been there.

"Unless I see him myself, I cannot believe it!" Thomas said.

The disciples only met together now behind locked doors. Yet somehow, suddenly, Jesus appeared. "Peace be with you," he greeted them.

Then he said, "Thomas, come here. Put your fingers in the nail marks. Feel for yourself the place in my side where they put the spear. Believe that I am alive!"

Falling to his knees, Thomas said, "My Lord and my God!"

Jesus ate and talked with them many times before he went back to be with God in heaven. Then he sent them the Holy Spirit, so that they would have the power to tell everyone all they knew about him.

Don't be afraid. Only believe.
Mark 5:36

Bible stories can be found as follows:

Published in the US by B&H Publishing Group
Nashville, TN
www.BHPublishingGroup.com
ISBN 978-0-8054-4647-0

Published in the UK by Anno Domini Publishing
1 Churchgates, The Wilderness,
Berkhamsted, Herts HP4 2UB England

First edition 2007

Copyright © 2007 Anno Domini Publishing
1 Churchgates, The Wilderness,
Berkhamsted, Herts HP4 2UB
Text copyright © 2007 Rhona Davies
Illustrations copyright © 2007 Tommaso d'incalci

Publishing Director Annette Reynolds
Editor Nicola Bull
Art Director Gerald Rogers
Pre-production Krystyna Kowalska Hewitt
Production John Laister

Scripture quotations have been taken from the Holman Christian
Standard Bible®, Copyright © 1999, 2000, 2002, 2003
by Holman Bible Publishers.

Printed and bound in Singapore